BIONICLE™

Legends
of Metru Nui

BIONICLE™

FIND THE POWER,
LIVE THE LEGEND

The legend comes alive in these exciting BIONICLE™ books:

BIONICLE™ Chronicles

#1 Tale of the Toa
#2 Beware the Bohrok
#3 Makuta's Revenge
#4 Tales of the Masks

The Official Guide to BIONICLE™

BIONICLE™ Collector's Sticker Book

BIONICLE™: Mask of Light

BIONICLE™ Adventures

#1 Mystery of Metru Nui
#2 Trial by Fire
#3 The Darkness Below

BIONICLE™

Legends of Metru Nui

by Greg Farshtey

SCHOLASTIC INC.
New York Toronto London Auckland Sydney
Mexico City New Delhi Hong Kong Buenos Aires

ISBN 0-439-62747-8

12 11 10 9 8 7 6 5 4 3 2 1   4 5 6 7 8/0

Printed in the U.S.A.
First printing, September 2004

*For Create TV and Film, Creative Capers, and Miramax
for bringing BIONICLE to life on the screen.*

The City of Metru Nui

BIONICLE™

Legends
of Metru Nui

INTRODUCTION

Turaga Vakama stood on a natural stone balcony that looked out over a vast silver sea. Directly in front of him was an Amaja circle, the sand pit used by Turaga for ages to tell stories of the past. Now, surrounded by his fellow Turaga, the Matoran villagers, the six Toa Nuva and Takanuva, Toa of Light, he was about to tell the most important tale of all.

"Gathered friends," he began. "Listen again to our legend of the Bionicle. In the time before time, in the glorious city of Metru Nui, we believed new heroes could not be made.

"But we were wrong."

Vakama moved the stone that represented the Great Spirit, Mata Nui, to the center of the circle. Now the lightstones began to flicker and darkness shrouded the sand pit.

"An unrelenting shadow sought to enforce endless sleep," Vakama continued, "until memories of times past were lost. Then he could create a time of dark order, and awaken the world as its conqueror."

Vakama raised his eyes to the heavens, remembering a time long ago. "Hope, it seemed, was lost."

Toa Lhikan, guardian of the city of Metru Nui, stood in the semi-darkness of the Great Temple. He had come here many times in the past to remember what had gone before and reflect on the future. This had always been a place that had soothed his spirit. But not today.

The errand that had brought him to one of the most revered sites in Metru Nui was one that filled him with sadness and doubt. Many a night he had wondered if there might be some other way, but no other answer presented itself. Finally, he admitted that he had no choice. It had to be done, and done now, before it was too late.

Grimly, Lhikan pried open the suva. Then he reached in and took the sixth and last Toa stone off its pedestal.

As he had done five times before, Toa Lhikan

placed the stone on a thin sheet of metallic protodermis in his open palm. Then he clenched his
fist, wrapping the sheet tightly around the stone.

Behind his yellow Great Mask of Shielding,
Lhikan's eyes narrowed. He knew that he was
doing far more than taking valuable objects of
power. He was taking a step that would change
his life, the lives of six others, and the very future
of Metru Nui.

He held his other hand over his closed fist
and concentrated. Six streams of energy came
from his hand, then merged into a single white
lance of power. It flowed over the wrapped Toa
stone, then abruptly came to a stop. When Lhikan
opened his fist, he saw that the metallic sheet was
now sealed around the stone. Imprinted upon it
was the symbol of the three virtues of the Matoran: Unity, Duty, and Destiny.

Lhikan heard a soft sound behind him and
turned quickly. Approaching from out of the
darkness were two figures, one a four-legged
insectoid being, the other a hulking brute. Lhikan

knew all too well who they were and why they were here. He was already moving as the insectoid began hurling energy blasts.

Fleeing was against Lhikan's nature, but he had been a Toa long enough to know it did not pay to challenge impossible odds. He ran, dodging as the two Dark Hunters attempted to snare him in energy webs. As they closed in, the Toa of Fire leaped through a window and plunged into space.

The insectoid Dark Hunter rushed to the window to watch his enemy fall. Instead, he saw Lhikan combine his tools to form a glider board. Seconds later, the Toa was lost from view.

Nokama stood near the Great Temple, surrounded by her students. As a teacher, she knew it was important to get her class out of the classroom now and then, and let them see some of Metru Nui's history for themselves. Using her trident, she pointed out some of the ancient carvings on the walls of the temple.

Behind her, she could hear her students gasp. She turned to see Toa Lhikan. He approached her, handed her a small package, and then was gone. Nokama shook her head, wondering what it could all mean.

In a Po-Metru assemblers' village, Onewa was hard at work finishing a piece of carving. He had been laboring in the heat all day, but hardly noticed the time or the effort. It was all worth it when the work was done and another fine display of craftsmanship was ready to ship out. He knew that each Po-Matoran crafter in the huts around him felt the same, except perhaps Ahkmou. That one seemed more worried about how many honors he would receive than how much work he finished.

Something landed with a sharp thud on the ground at Onewa's feet. It was a small package wrapped in what looked like foil. Onewa looked up just in time to see the departing form of Toa Lhikan.

*   *   *

6

Whenua was content. A new shipment of Bohrok had arrived at the Archives. As soon as he was done cataloging the creatures, they would be ready to go on exhibit for all Matoran to see.

He worked quickly, sorting through the items in a pile of artifacts. Some were slated for immediate exhibit, others would be sent down to the sublevels, and still more were too damaged to be of any use. These would be sent to Ta-Metru to be melted down.

Whenua was so absorbed by his work that he never heard Toa Lhikan's approach. The Toa paused only long enough to hand the Matoran a small object, then he was gone. Whenua looked in wonder at the package, whose covering glittered even in the dim light of the Archives.

Matau took a deep breath. This was his favorite part of the job — testing new vehicles before they hit the streets of Le-Metru. He was, naturally, the best qualified to run them around the test track, being the most highly skilled rider in the entire metru . . . at least, in his opinion.

Today's test vehicle was a one-Matoran moto-sled invented by an Onu-Matoran named Nuparu. He claimed it would someday replace the Ussal crabs that carried cargo to and fro in Metru Nui. Matau was less worried about that than about how fast it could go.

When the signal was given, Matau worked the controls and the machine began to move. Soon it was racing around the test track. Matau smiled, certain that he could coax a little more speed out of Nuparu's machine. He reached out, grabbed one of the controls — and it broke off in his hand.

Matau's eyes went wide. *Oh, this is not happy-cheer at all,* he thought.

All around him, pieces of the vehicle were flying off as the vehicle spun madly. Finally, only the control seat remained, with Matau hanging on to keep from being tossed the length of the track. Sparks flew as the lone intact section skidded to a halt, while Matau leaped off at the last possible moment.

The Matoran managed not to break anything on his landing. As he rose to his feet, he saw he was not alone. Toa Lhikan was standing beside him, offering him a gift. Then the Toa was gone.

Matau looked at the small, heavy item in his hand. *Truly an ever-strange day*, he said to himself.

Nuju peered through his telescope. From his vantage point high atop a Ko-Metru tower, he could see the sky, the stars, Toa Lhikan gliding toward him —

Toa Lhikan?

The lone protector of Metru Nui landed softly beside the Matoran. Without a word, he handed Nuju a wrapped Toa stone. Then, secure that the coast was clear, Lhikan leaped from the roof and surfed away on the wind.

Nuju watched him go, wondering what this event might mean for his future.

Vakama carefully moved a Kanoka disk from his worktable into the fires of the forge. He watched intently as the flames softened the disk. When he felt the time was right, he removed it from the heat and began to shape it with his firestaff. He smoothed the rough edges of the disk, added eyeholes, and then paused to look at the Mask of Power he had created.

Far below him, a pool of molten protodermis bubbled and hissed. This was the raw material that was fed into the forge to be shaped into disks, and later into masks, if the grade of disk was high enough. All around was a series of interlocking catwalks, with a great crane suspended above the center of the molten vat.

Vakama held the mask up to the light and searched for flaws in the workmanship. Finding none, he placed it on his face. Given that it was a Great Mask, he knew he would not be able to access its powers, but he could at least get a sense of whether it was active. But when he donned it, it merely glowed dimly before flickering out.

Disgusted, Vakama took it off and threw it on top of a huge pile of similar masks. At the rate he was going, his stack of failures would soon be taller than he was. Shaking his head, he turned to see Toa Lhikan standing before him.

"Making Great Masks, Vakama?" asked the Toa.

Vakama took a step backward and stumbled. "Toa Lhikan! Um, not yet . . . but with the right disk . . ."

"The city needs your help," said Lhikan, reaching behind him to retrieve something. A moment later Vakama saw it was a small package wrapped in a shiny material.

"My help?" the Matoran said, taking another step backward. He bumped into the discard pile, causing the rejected masks to clatter to the floor.

"Matoran are vanishing," Lhikan continued urgently. "Deceit lurks in the shadows of Metru Nui."

"Toa — so dramatic."

Both Lhikan and Vakama turned at the voice. A large, four-legged, insectoid creature stood inside the foundry. "Always playing the hero," the creature hissed.

"Some of us take our duty seriously, Nid-hiki," growled Lhikan. Then he turned to Vakama, gestured to the package, and whispered, "Keep it safe. Get to the Great Temple."

Nidhiki raised his claws. "This time your farewell will be forever, brother."

"You lost the right to call me brother long ago," said Lhikan.

Nidhiki spat blasts of dark energy. Lhikan narrowly evaded them, but one surge of energy struck the support for the catwalk, shearing through it. Lhikan was considering his next move when there came a crash from above. He looked up to see a mammoth form falling toward him.

"Time's up, Toa!" bellowed the plummeting figure.

Nidhiki smiled as his bestial partner, Krekka, crashed onto the catwalk beside Lhikan. Immediately, Toa and Dark Hunter began to grapple. Krekka's size and strength gave him the edge, but in Lhikan he faced the veteran of a thousand conflicts. The Toa waited for the right moment, then sidestepped and used Krekka's force against him. With one smooth motion, Lhikan tossed Krekka over the side of the catwalk.

The Dark Hunter might not have been the brightest being in Metru Nui, but even he knew what would happen if he landed in the vat of molten protodermis. His hand shot out and grabbed onto the edge of the catwalk, and he began to pull himself back up.

Lhikan glanced toward Vakama. The Matoran had been watching the struggle, so frozen with shock that he had not noticed the damage done by Nidhiki's earlier blast. But Lhikan could see that the catwalk on which Vakama stood was about to collapse.

"Vakama! Move!" he shouted.

It was already too late. Metal groaned and snapped and the catwalk broke free of its supports, sending Vakama sliding toward molten doom. Ignoring the threat of Nidhiki, Lhikan jumped to the broken platform and grabbed hold of the Matoran.

Nidhiki's eyes narrowed. "Compassion was always your weakness, brother," he said.

Lhikan struggled to haul Vakama back up to relative safety. Then he suddenly felt himself seized and lifted into the air. The Toa turned to see that Krekka had taken control of the crane, and it was that which now dangled Lhikan and Vakama over the bubbling vat. "It's swim time!" snarled Krekka.

The Dark Hunter shifted the controls and began to lower the crane toward the vat. Lhikan summoned all his strength, and hoisted Vakama high so the Matoran could grab onto the clawlike end of the crane. "Don't let go," the Toa ordered.

"Wasn't planning to," Vakama replied.

That had been the easy part. Now Toa Lhikan started to swing his body back and forth like a pendulum, trying to build up enough force to execute his only possible plan. He didn't think about what would happen if he failed, or about the molten substance waiting below — his entire focus was on the timing and speed of his swing.

At the crucial moment, Lhikan let go of the

crane and went sailing through the air. He landed on top of the machine's cab, much to the surprise of Krekka. Before the Dark Hunter could react, Lhikan had shouldered him aside and stopped the crane's descent.

The Toa had no chance to celebrate his triumph. An energy web launched by Nidhiki wrapped around Lhikan, trapping him. As he struggled in vain to escape, his eyes locked on the Matoran.

"Vakama, the Great Spirit depends on you!" he cried. "Save the heart of Metru Nui!"

Krekka released an arc of dark energy that bound the Toa's hands, but Vakama could no longer see. His mind had been overtaken by a vision of the future. . . .

Time slowing, slowing, almost coming to a stop. A face coming closer, but obscured by waves of elemental energy. Now it became clearer . . . it was Lhikan . . . but twisted and distorted . . . and behind him, a pair of red eyes that radiated pure evil . . .

The horrifying sight snapped Vakama out of his trance, but left him weak and trembling. He glanced around dazedly, and was just in time to see Lhikan being dragged off by Krekka and Nidhiki. "Time is short!" yelled Lhikan. "Stop the darkness!"

"No!" Vakama shouted. For, in truth, there was nothing else he could do.

Near the Fountains of Wisdom in Ga-Metru, scores of Matoran looked up at a massive screen. The wise, benevolent mask of Turaga Dume, elder of the city, gazed down upon them. None paid any attention to the transport that crawled by on insectoid legs. Driven by Vahki Bordakh, the order enforcement squads of Ga-Metru, it carried several large, silver spheres.

"Matoran of Metru Nui," Dume began, his voice and image carried all over the city. "It is with deep sorrow that I must inform you of the disappearance of our beloved Toa Lhikan."

In Ko-Metru, Ta-Metru, and all around the city, Matoran gasped. Those who attempted to approach the screen, or turn away from it, were stopped by Vahki squads.

"But with the help of the Vahki," Dume

continued, "order shall be maintained. Trust in me and soon all your concerns will be laid to rest."

The Turaga's words felt like hot irons to Vakama. Back in his forge, he was looking at the package Lhikan had given to him.

"Toa Lhikan . . . I failed you," he said sadly. He undid the foil wrapping to find he was holding a Toa stone. It was then he noticed the writing on the metal wrapping, but before he could examine it more closely —

"You should not blame yourself, Vakama."

The Matoran turned to see Turaga Dume entering, flanked by a squad of Vahki. A good mask-height taller than Vakama, Dume radiated wisdom and a paternal feeling for all Matoran. But the Vahki close by were a constant reminder that Dume was *the* authority in Metru Nui and his words were to be obeyed.

Dume looked around at the chaos left in the wake of Lhikan's struggle with the Dark Hunters. "You are a mask-maker, not a Toa," he said gently.

Vakama nodded. While Dume was looking away, he slipped the Toa stone and its wrapping onto the already cluttered table behind him. Certain it was well hidden, he went to get a chair for Dume, only to get his feet tangled and stumble to the ground.

"I have come for the Mask of Time," said Dume.

Vakama scrambled to his feet. "Yes, ah, well . . . I am sorry, Turaga. It's not yet ready. Great Masks take time to craft."

"Perhaps you are using inferior disks."

"I use the finest quality available, Turaga. Only Great Disks are more pure, but they can only be retrieved by a Toa."

Dume turned away. "Of course. Pity Toa Lhikan is not here to help."

Vakama turned and bumped the table, knocking the Toa stone off. Only swift movement let him catch it and conceal it again before Dume turned back to him.

"Bring the completed mask to the Coliseum before the great contest," the Turaga ordered. "The destiny of Metru Nui rests in your hands."

Vakama allowed himself a sigh of relief as

the Turaga and his Vahki departed. As soon as they were out of sight, he went back to the metal wrapping. On closer examination he could see the writing on it was a detailed map — a map of a place every Matoran knew well.

"The Great Temple . . ." Vakama whispered.

As soon as he was able, Vakama slipped away and journeyed to Ga-Metru. But when he arrived at the Great Temple, he found to his surprise that there were other Matoran there as well. Five of them, in fact, and all strangers to him.

Matau looked Vakama up and down and said, "Fire-spitter? Did you wrong-turn?"

"You tell me," Vakama replied, opening his hand to reveal the Toa stone he carried.

Nokama stepped forward and showed that she, too, had a Toa stone. Each of the other Matoran did the same. "It seems we are all recipients of Toa Lhikan's gifts. All similar, yet each unique."

"Like us!" said Matau, smiling. "All Matoran — some just more handsome than the rest."

Whenua shook his head. "Who's ever heard of Matoran getting summoned to the Great Temple like this?"

"What will be asked of us?" added Nuju. "We are all just . . . strangers."

"Some stranger than others," said Onewa.

Nokama gave the Po-Matoran a sharp look. "Your negativity pollutes this sanctuary, builder."

"Save the lessons for your class, teacher," Onewa spat back.

Their argument was interrupted by the sudden appearance of a stone shrine, which rose out of the floor in front of them. "The Toa Suva!" exclaimed Vakama.

"When Toa realize their full potential, this suva shrine grants them their elemental powers," Whenua recited from memory.

Each of the Matoran stepped forward and placed their Toa stone in a niche in the suva. A beam of elemental energy shot from the assembled stones. The temple chamber shook as if a great earthquake had struck the city. Then, as suddenly as they began, the tremors came to a stop.

The Matoran looked at one another, bewildered, as the image of Toa Lhikan's mask appeared in the energy beam. The yellow Kanohi Hau hovered in the air.

"Faithful Matoran, Metru Nui needs you," the Hau said, speaking in Lhikan's voice. "A shadow threatens its heart. Prove yourselves worthy Toa and fear not. The Great Spirit shall guide you in ways you could not imagine."

The mask glowed blindingly bright. The Matoran staggered backward as beams of energy shot from the mask, bathing them in unimaginable power. The Matoran began to glow, then change. Their bodies grew taller and stronger, armor forming where none had been before. Their masks transformed from the simple Kanohi of Matoran into Great Masks of Power.

The hovering mask, now a bright ball of light, suddenly winked out. No sign of its presence remained, not even the Toa stones. The six Matoran — now six armored Toa Metru — looked at themselves and each other in awe.

"Are we . . . Toa?" asked Onewa, excitement in his voice.

"If we appear to be Toa-heroes, then we are Toa-heroes!" answered Matau.

Whenua shook his head. "Since when are Matoran just zapped into Toa?"

"When uncertain times lie ahead," suggested Nuju.

Onewa looked around. "Now all we need are —"

As if in answer, the sides of the raised suva fell away to reveal a cache of Toa tools. "These!" shouted Matau.

The six new Toa rushed over to choose their equipment. Onewa grabbed a pair of proto pitons, Nuju twin crystal spikes, and Whenua earthshock drills. Vakama pondered for a moment before taking a disk launcher for himself.

"Nice choice . . . for playing Matoran games, mask-maker," chuckled Matau.

Nokama chose a pair of hydro blades, even as Matau began practicing with his aero slicers. He executed a series of rapid maneuvers with the sharp tools, shouting, "Oh yeah!" Halfway through a particularly complicated exercise, one of the blades flew from his hand and narrowly missed the new Toa Metru of Water.

"Need I remind you," snapped Nokama, "this is about honoring our responsibilities to the Great Spirit?"

"Nokama is right," agreed Whenua. "Maskmaker, you saw Toa Lhikan last, right?"

When Vakama nodded, Nuju said, "What did he say we could expect?"

Hesitantly, Vakama took a step forward. "He said . . ." the Toa Metru of Fire whispered.

"Speak up, fire-spitter!" said Onewa.

"He told me to stop the darkness . . . that I had to save the heart of Metru Nui," Vakama replied. "Then the Dark Hunters took him away . . . it was because of me."

Vakama stopped speaking. His thoughts had turned inward as another vision overtook him.

Shadows criss-crossed the landscape. Vakama was leading a group of figures toward Metru Nui, when there was a bright flash. It illuminated a city in ruins! Stunned, Vakama moved forward, only to see the city suddenly restored before his eyes.

Six Kanoka Disks flew toward him. Vakama ducked and dodged to avoid being struck, but the disks were not trying to harm him. Instead, they merged together to form one huge disk before bursting brilliantly into —

Then Vakama was back with the other Toa. Though the vision was gone, he was still shielding his eyes from the flash of light. Onewa looked at him and said, "All that smelting must have cooked his head."

"I saw it!" Vakama said frantically. "Metru Nui was destroyed! The six Great Kanoka Disks were headed right for me."

"Thanks for dream-sharing," said Matau, making no effort to keep the doubt out of his voice.

"Finding them would prove to Turaga Dume we are worthy Toa," insisted Vakama.

"Well, according to ancient legend, one Great Disk is hidden in each metru," said Whenua.

"So we go on a scavenger hunt because a fire-spitter stood too long in front of his forge?" sneered Onewa.

"Visions can be a sign of madness," said Nokama. "Or messages from the Great Spirit. But as Toa, we cannot afford to ignore them."

When no one spoke, she continued. "Then it is agreed. Each will recover the Great Disk from our own metru and present it to Turaga Dume."

Onewa looked at Vakama and muttered, "I am doing this for Lhikan. No one else."

Nokama led the Toa Metru deeper into the temple. On one wall was an ancient carving that the Toa of Water said contained clues to the locations of the six Great Disks.

"The Great Disks will be found by seeking the unfamiliar within the familiar . . ." she read.

In Po-Metru, you must seek a mountain in balance. . . .
High above the Sculpture Fields of Po-

Metru, Onewa, Toa of Stone, wrestled to free the Great Disk. The disk was embedded in a huge, triangular slab of protodermis that was delicately balanced on one point. With a mighty heave, he freed the disk — and the slab began to topple toward him. . . .

In Ko-Metru, find where the sky and ice are joined. . . .

Nuju, Toa Metru of Ice, slid down a steep incline, headed for a very long fall. As he flew off the edge of the Knowledge Tower roof, Nuju grabbed on to a huge icicle that hung from the ledge. That was when he noticed that this icicle was most unusual.

Frozen inside it was a Great Disk.

The Great Disk of Le-Metru will be all around you when you find it. . . .

Matau, Toa of Air, was in the one place he always hoped to avoid: inside a magnetic force sphere hurtling through a Le-Matoran transport chute toward certain destruction. But the sphere, which absorbed any debris around it, had also captured the Great Disk and unless Matau retrieved it, the disk would be shattered.

Some days, being a Toa-hero is not all it's cracked up to be, he said to himself.

No door must be left unopened in Onu-Metru. . . .

Whenua struggled to slam a door in the Archives. The angry mutant Ussal crab on the other side had other ideas, though. Its massive claw snapped, trying to trap the Toa of Earth in its pincers. Not for the first time, Whenua wished that they would put signs on the doors of the exhibit rooms in this living museum.

Using all of his Toa strength, Whenua succeeded in shutting and locking the massive door. He looked at the Great Disk in his hand and hoped that in the end all this struggle would be worth it.

In Ga-Metru, go beyond the depths of any Toa before. . . .

Nokama swam through the protodermis

sea with smooth, easy strokes. She had success-
fully wrestled the Great Disk from between two
jagged outcroppings and now was headed to the
surface with it.

She had been so excited about finding it
that she never noticed that the two "outcroppings" were teeth . . . or that a huge creature from
the ocean's depths was now closing in on her. . . .

Embrace the root of fire in Ta-Metru . . .
Vakama hung suspended in a Ta-Metru fire
pit, trapped in the grip of a blackened, twisted
plant. In his hand he clutched a Great Disk . . . but
just how he would make it out of the pit with
disk intact, he could not imagine.

And these glorious disks will be yours.
After many adventures, both together and
separately, the Toa Metru finally met outside the
Coliseum. Each held the Great Disk from his or
her own metru.

Nokama looked at her fellow Toa Metru.
"Any troubles?"

The Toa looked at the ground, at the Coliseum, at anything but each other. "No," each mumbled in turn.

Then they walked together toward the massive door of the Metru Nui Coliseum.

The Coliseum towered over the city. It stood at the junction of all six metru, so tall it looked as if it must touch the sky. The Coliseum was large enough to accommodate every Matoran in Metru Nui, and served as both an athletic arena and the power station for the entire city. Turaga Dume's chambers were also to be found in this imposing building. One side of the arena was dominated by a massive statue of Toa Lhikan, the other by Dume's box.

The Toa Metru entered the arena in the middle of a Kanoka Disk tournament. All around them Matoran surfed on disks, over the undulating floor trying to launch their Kanoka into hoops mounted high on the walls. When the players saw the visitors, they immediately ceased their game and moved aside. The floor of the arena settled back into its natural bowl shape.

Great Disks held high, the Toa Metru moved into the middle of the stadium. Quietly at first, the crowd began to chant "Toa . . . Toa . . . Toa . . ." Then the word burst from them in a cheer that rocked the Coliseum.

"Hello, Metru Nui!" Matau shouted, waving. Then he turned to the other Toa, saying, "I always wanted to loud-shout that!"

From high in his box, Turaga Dume watched the arrival of the Toa with surprise. He was flanked by two Vahki Rorzakh from Onu-Metru, and his huge, powerful hawk, Nivawk, perched behind him.

Dume leaned forward and said in disbelief, "Vakama?!" Regaining control of himself with some effort, he continued, "Matoran in the morning. Toa by afternoon. No wonder you have not yet completed the Mask of Time."

"Forgive the delay, Turaga, but . . ." Vakama began.

"One moment we're Matoran, the next we're power-jolted," shouted Matau, shaking his body to simulate the shock. "And Toa-masked!"

Nokama held her Great Disk up, followed by the others, and said to Dume, "We present you the Great Kanoka Disks as proof of our Toa stature."

"Toa must prove themselves with deeds, not simple gifts," Dume replied. Then, addressing the crowd, he said, "Matoran of Metru Nui! The Great Spirit has provided six new Toa who will undoubtedly demonstrate their worthiness on this field of honor!"

The crowd cheered, but the Toa Metru just stood there, stunned. All that work to retrieve the Great Disks, and Turaga Dume rejected them? One by one, they handed the disks to Vakama, disappointment and scorn on their faces. This had been his idea, and it had not worked.

"Catch this, fire-spitter," Onewa snapped.

In the Coliseum's control box, Matoran busily worked a series of levers and switches. The Toa Metru could hear machinery grinding and clanking beneath their feet. Then Dume's face appeared on the giant screen overlooking the field.

"Cross the Sea of Protodermis," he boomed, "and be honored as Toa!"

The field began to move, shift, undulate beneath the Toa Metru. They struggled to keep their balance as wave after wave passed through the ground. Then a series of large, silver columns topped with razor-sharp points erupted randomly out of the field, threatening to skewer the Toa.

Matau narrowly avoided the first thrust, saying, "Lucky I'm so quick-fast!" But that left Nuju in harm's way. The Toa Metru of Ice leaped back, crashing into Whenua and sending them both to the ground.

"How will we survive?" asked Nuju.

"We use the mask powers the Great Spirit gave us!" answered Whenua.

"And just how do we do that?!"

There was no time for a reply as more columns shot out of the ground. Back on his feet, Nuju pivoted out of the way of a pair of them, not realizing where he was swinging his crystal spike. His Toa tool swept the legs out from under Vakama, sending the Toa of Fire to the ground. The crowd began to laugh.

Vakama shook off the impact and looked

up to see a tidal wave of solid protodermis heading right for the Toa. He jumped to his feet as Nokama pointed to an archway on the far side of the field.

"Follow me!" she shouted, leading the charge toward safety.

The huge swell rose behind them, but the Toa were able to maintain their balance and slide down the side of the wave. But now more swells rose up in front of them, each larger than the last. One lifted Whenua high into the air and then dropped him on the field in a heap.

More swells pounded the Toa from every side. Even as Onewa barely dodged a twenty-five-foot tidal wave of protodermis, another hurled Nuju, Vakama, and Nokama in separate directions. Then the largest wave of all rose before them, moving forward at alarming speed and breaking up into large blocks of metal.

"Time to quick-run!" Matau yelled.

"Advance!" Nuju yelled.

"No, retreat!" said Whenua, charging backward and colliding with the Toa of Ice. They both looked up in time to see the blocks of protodermis raining down. Only swift reflexes saved them from being crushed.

"Enough!" proclaimed Dume. The Matoran in the control box dutifully shut down the field.

The Toa Metru were scattered all over the field, exhausted. The crowd was silent. Dume peered down at the six figures and smiled.

"Let us praise these jesters," he said. "Perhaps they thought to entertain us during this difficult time . . ."

"No!" shouted Vakama. "We are Toa!"

"Or are they impostors responsible for Toa Lhikan's demise?" continued Dume. "Vakama here was the last to see him!"

"Yes, but . . . no . . . not true!" Vakama stammered.

Dume's face leered down from the giant screen. "Seize them!"

Vakama's eyes widened as he saw Krekka and Nidhiki step up beside Turaga Dume. Could it be . . . ?

"No, it was them!" he yelled, pointing at the two Dark Hunters. "They did it!"

Squads of Rorzakh closed in on the Toa, their staffs at the ready. The Matoran in the control box flipped more switches, converting the center of the field into a vast, metallic whirlpool. Closest to the center of the vortex, Whenua, Nuju, and Onewa struggled to resist the pull.

Nuju tried to dig his crystal spike into the ground, but the force of the whirlpool tore it from his hands and it plunged into the darkness. Seconds later, Nuju joined it, flying headlong toward the vortex. On the way, he smashed into Whenua, sending the Toa of Earth plummeting into the whirlpool as well.

Matau and Nokama plunged their tools into the protodermis to try and fight the pull. Vakama came flying toward them, but Nokama seized him at the last moment with her free hand.

Onewa was not so fortunate. With a scream of "Help!" he vanished into the whirlpool.

Nokama looked around. The Rorzakh

were closing in and the three remaining Toa were helpless. Then her eyes fixed on the statue of Toa Lhikan.

"Vakama!" she shouted, pointing toward the sculpture. "The statue! Bring it down!"

The Toa of Fire nodded and went to load a disk into his disk launcher. He was half done when he realized he had one of the Great Disks in his hand. Thinking better of it, he substituted disks from his pack.

Taking as careful aim as he could under the circumstances, Vakama launched a series of disks at the base of the statue. Half of the disks contained the weakness power, half the reconstitute at random power — the combination was explosive, sending the sculpture toppling to the ground. Rorzakh scattered in its wake, some of them drawn into the vortex, others trapped beneath the weight of the statue.

"Go! Now!" said Nokama.

The three Toa scrambled over the statue, past the stunned Rorzakh, and out of the Coliseum. As they ran, Matau stole a glance at

Vakama's disk launcher. "Impressive Toa tool," he said. "Trade?"

But Vakama was not listening. His attention, and his anger, were fixed on the Turaga of his city.

Dume turned to Nidhiki and Krekka, barely controlled anger in his voice. "The new Toa must not interfere with the plan."

Nidhiki shrugged. "They are mere Matoran in Toa armor. As is our duty, we shall not fail."

Krekka pondered that for a long moment before nodding his agreement.

Outside the Coliseum, the three Toa Metru paused to catch their breath. Vakama's mind was still spinning from the revelation that Dume, Nidhiki, and Krekka were allies.

"The Dark Hunters took Toa Lhikan — for Turaga Dume! He's responsible!" he said.

Nokama nodded. "And now he'll send them after us."

"All because the fire-spitter panic-failed,"

grumbled Matau. He remembered all too well what Vakama had said about standing by while Toa Lhikan was kidnapped.

Vakama made no reply. There was nothing he could say.

"We have to get out of here," said Nokama. She looked down to see a transport chute far below. Jumping into one was risky. If the speed and timing of the leap were not just right, she would bounce off the outer layer rather than passing through into the magnetized protodermis flow.

Taking a deep breath, she jumped off the ledge. An experienced diver, she kept her body as straight as could be and her eyes focused on her destination. She struck the chute perfectly, passing through the outer layer and immediately swimming smoothly in the chute.

High above, Vakama watched her dive with awe and not a little fear. Ta-Matoran didn't go leaping around like Le-Metru cable climbers or swimming in the sea like Ruki fish. Vakama had never gotten into a chute except through a chute station. Besides being dangerous, it was a sure way to attract the attention of Vahki.

Behind him, Matau grew impatient. He gave Vakama a shove and sent the Toa of Fire flying. Fortunately, he hit the chute at just the right moment and made it into the protodermis flow safely. It took him a moment to adjust to the new environment. He grabbed a passing piece of cargo and let it pull him along behind Nokama.

Matau turned at a noise behind him. Krekka and Nidhiki had emerged from the Coliseum. At the sight of the Toa, they shapeshifted into a more aerodynamic mode and shot forward. Panicked, Matau leaped.

Under ordinary circumstances, the Le-Metru native was one of the best at chute-jumping. But he had never tried to do it with two Dark Hunters right behind him before. His arms and legs were going every which way as he fell. He landed with a hard splat on the top of the chute, then slowly oozed into the protodermis.

Part of him was happy for the temporary safety, while part hoped no one he knew had seen him.

Turaga Dume walked silently through his private chamber. Despite the numerous lightstone lanterns, the vast room still felt shadowy and cold. Ignoring the great throne that rested on the polished floor, Dume triggered a secret door in the rear wall and passed through.

Beyond the door was a room no eyes other than his own had ever seen. Sunlight poured into the room from either side to strike a pair of huge sundials. The instruments were made of great circular plates inscribed with a language that was ancient when Metru Nui was new, and posts of a dark stone that cast eerie shadows. The plates rotated with a rhythmic clicking, bringing the shadows from the sundial posts closer and closer with each second.

Turaga Dume walked toward the darkest recesses of the room. A pair of sinister red eyes loomed in the shadows before him. A voice like thunder growled from the pit, "The Mask of Time will not be completed."

"No," said Turaga Dume. "But when the Great Shadow falls, the Vahki will ensure every Matoran's fate."

The eyes receded into the darkness. The room was silent as the grave once more.

Toa Nokama twisted her body to avoid slamming into a freight sled. Behind her, Vakama and Matau did the same while trying to maintain their grip on items flying through the chutes. It was the height of the Metru Nui traffic rush and freight convoys were roaring by at alarming speeds.

Still, her Toa strength and agility made it a task she could handle. The real challenge was figuring out where in Metru Nui to go that the Vahki could not follow.

Inside the Le-Metru control room that governed the chutes, a very frightened Matoran looked for help — but there was none coming. The Matoran's name was Kongu, and in ages of work he had never run into anything more dangerous

than the occasional force sphere or chute break-
down. Now, held in the grip of the Dark Hunter
called Krekka, he knew the true meaning of fear.

"The entire system will explode if I reverse
the flow!" he cried.

In the background, Nidhiki hissed. Krekka
raised a powerful arm so that Kongu could get a
hint of his fate if he refused to cooperate.

"Then again, it might work," Kongu said
weakly. His hand slammed on a button, and with a
great *whoosh* the magnetized protodermis pumps
that powered the chutes began to reverse.

The Toa's journey came to an abrupt halt. All forward motion stopped in the chutes at once, leav-
ing heroes, Matoran, and freight sleds hanging
suspended in the energy field. Vakama and Matau
looked at each other and shrugged.

Then, with an earsplitting roar, the flow of
the chutes suddenly reversed itself. The Toa tumbled backward, out of control, smashing into the
walls as the transport system picked up speed.
There was nothing to grab on to, no way to gain

traction. Even thinking was difficult with the constant collisions.

Nokama somersaulted end over end, catching a glimpse of a freight sled spinning madly and heading in her direction. At the last moment, she and the other Toa flattened themselves against the walls and took only glancing blows from the vehicle.

This can't go on, thought Nokama. *It's only a matter of time before something strikes us . . . or worse, we end up back where we started, in the hands of the Vahki.*

With that fate in mind, Nokama dug her twin hydro blades into the bottom of the chute. Holding on to the blades with one hand, she grabbed Vakama with the other. Then Vakama grabbed Matau, linking them all together in a chain.

His motion stabilized, Matau freed his aero slicer and carved a hole in the bottom of the tube. He looked up to see another out-of-control freight sled bearing down on them. In the instant before it would have struck, the three Toa plunged through the hole and into space.

Now they hung in mid-air, high above Metru Nui. Nokama clung to her hydro blades, while Vakama held on to her ankle. With his free hand, he clutched Matau.

"Everyone all right?" asked Nokama.

Matau looked up from where he dangled above the city. "Oh, sure-fine," he said sarcastically. "Just enjoying the view."

Nokama looked down at Vakama. The Toa of Fire was staring off into space. "Vakama?" she said.

But Vakama was no longer there, at least not in his mind. He was lost in another vision. . . .

He was standing next to Toa Lhikan. But as Vakama moved to greet his lost friend, the Toa suddenly transformed into a blinding burst of energy. The sphere of light hovered in the air for a moment before launching skyward.

Vakama lifted his gaze to watch it streak across the night sky. As it sped across the blackness, the energy field shifted and changed until it resembled the shooting stars studied by Ko-Metru scholars. But it was no random astronomical event — no, it looked more like an arrow pointing toward . . .

With a start, Vakama snapped out of his trance. Nokama was looking down at him, concerned.

"Another foreseeing?" asked the Toa of Water.

Vakama nodded, a little embarrassed.

"How about less vision-seeing and more Toa-saving?" shouted Matau.

Nokama glanced up to see that her hydro blades were losing their grip on the chute. Fighting to stay calm, she began to swing, the movement of her body forcing the other Toa to move as well. Slowly they gained momentum, arcing toward a nearby support tower and then back again. With each swing, the hydro blades lost a bit more of their grip.

At the apex of the next swing, the Toa tools suddenly came loose. Nokama hurled herself through the air and grabbed onto the support tower. But the jolt rocked Vakama and Matau, causing the Toa of Fire to lose his grip. The Toa of Air plunged toward the ground far below.

"Matau!" cried Vakama.

But the Toa of Air could not hear him over the sound of the wind rushing in his ears. Arms and legs outstretched, he was desperately wishing he had mastered his Great Mask of Power. *Unless, of course, it was a useless-dumb power like water breathing,* he thought. *But if it was something like levitation, that would be really welcome-fine right now. . . .*

Even as the thought crossed his mind, his fall became a controlled glide. His aero slicers caught the wind, acting like wings. A broad grin broke out on Matau's face.

"My mask power!" he yelled happily. "I can —"

The updraft became a downdraft without warning, sending Matau crashing headfirst into a massive screen. "Unnngh! Wind-fly," he groaned.

As he slid down the screen, Turaga Dume's face glared down from it. "All Matoran should be on the lookout for the false Toa," ordered the elder of Metru Nui.

Up above, Nokama felt her heart sink.

Somehow, she did not think this was what Lhikan had in mind when he gave them the Toa stones.

Nokama took a swift look around. No, there were no Vahki Keerakh in the area, or even many Matoran, for that matter. This seemed like a safe spot for the three Toa Metru to pause and try to sort out what had just happened.

Matau spent the time recovering from his first "solo flight." Nokama had made a point of not teasing him about it, since the Toa of Air seemed to feel bad enough already. Vakama was off by himself, doing something with a pair of Great Disks.

Nokama approached in time to see him move the disks together until they touched. Then something strange happened — the disks softened and began to merge together. Vakama quickly pulled them apart again, puzzled and intrigued.

"Vakama?"

"Huh?" said the Toa of Fire, not looking up.

"What was your last vision?" Nokama asked.

Vakama pointed up to the sky. A yellow streak of light could be seen against the blackness. "That! Toa Lhikan's spirit star. Each Toa has one. As long as it burns in the night sky, Toa Lhikan remains alive."

"It is headed toward Po-Metru," said Nokama.

Matau had joined the group now. He glanced up at the spirit star, shrugged, and said, "What about our captured Toa-brothers?"

Vakama shook his head. "Only Toa Lhikan can stop Turaga Dume and free the other Toa."

"And how do you propose we quick-catch a spirit star?" demanded Matau.

Nokama scanned the area. Down the road, she spotted a Vahki transport vehicle moving slowly through the metru. The long vehicle was propelled by a series of insectlike legs. Its cargo was a collection of large silver spheres. Only a single Vahki was present, serving as driver.

"Perhaps a way has been revealed, rider," Nokama said, smiling.

Toa of Water and Toa of Air took off at a

run for the transport. When they had gone a few steps, Nokama looked back to see that Vakama hadn't moved. He was still toying with the two Great Disks.

"Vakama!" she shouted.

Startled, Vakama returned the disks to his backpack and ran to catch up. As the transport rumbled by, the three of them leaped into the back without being seen. They settled themselves down between tall stacks of silver spheres, the like of which none of them had ever seen before.

"What are these?" wondered Vakama.

"Storage containers," replied Matau. "But most odd-looking."

Vakama brushed his hand against one of the spheres, and his mind exploded . . .

Without warning, the sphere sprung open, revealing a Matoran in a coma-like slumber. The next moment, the Matoran's heartlight faded to black. Before Vakama could react, the Matoran's mask began to blur and morph, transforming into that of Turaga Dume. A pair of red eyes blazed at Vakama from Dume's Kanohi mask. . . .

The Toa of Fire returned to reality with a start. Another vision . . . and if it were true . . .

He shoved Matau aside to get at the nearest sphere. "Hey! Are you cross-wired?" Matau snapped.

Vakama threw the sphere open to find . . . nothing. Nokama joined him to peer into the empty container. "What's wrong, brother?" she asked.

The Toa of Fire stared hard at the darkness in the heart of the sphere. "Nothing, sister. Nothing at all," he said finally.

Matau met Nokama's eyes and spun his hand around, a not-so-subtle way of saying Vakama was crazy. Nokama frowned, part of her wishing she could believe that. It would make things much simpler. But deep down she had a feeling that the situation in Metru Nui was far worse than any of them knew . . . except, perhaps, Vakama.

▲ Vakama rides a wave of molten protodermis.

Vhisola and Nokama stand by one of Ga-Metru's canals. ▼

Onewa searches for a Great Disk of Power. ▲

▼ **Nuju leaps from a Knowledge Tower.**

Matau is handed a Kanoka disk by a Matoran. ▲

▼ Whenua saves a Matoran who has gotten into trouble.

Toa Lhikan, protector of Matu Nui and all the Matoran. ▲

▼ Toa Lhikan gives Vakama a mysterious package.

Matau drives a Vahki transport. ▲

▼ **The Dark Hunters search for the Toa.**

The false Dume transformed. ▲

▼**The Toa Metru encounter a mysterious Turaga.**

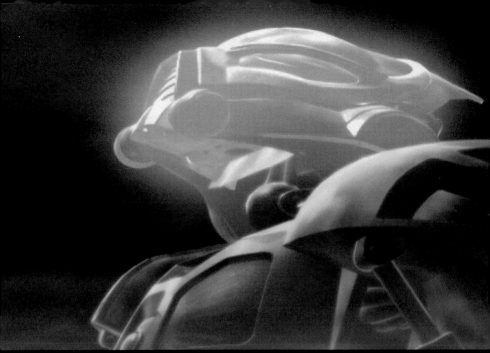

Vakama wears the Mask of Time. ▲

▼ The Toa stand united.

▲ **The Toa combine powers.**

An uncertain future awaits. ▼

5

To Whenua, it didn't seem like things could get any worse. He, Nuju, and Onewa had awakened in a cell, complete with thick rock walls and a solid metal door. Their Toa tools were missing. Worse, not only were they trapped, but they were being tortured by each other's company.

For the sixth time in the last two minutes, Whenua tried the door. It was still locked tight. "This is just great," he growled. "Before, when I woke up, all I worried about was cataloging. Now I will go down in history as Metru Nui's most wanted."

Onewa studied the stone walls. His time as a carver had helped him master the art of finding weak points in rock. But this cell did not seem to have any. Whenua's complaints only added to his frustration. "You? I'm the one suffering, locked up with a Ko-Matoran big brain and an Onu-Matoran stock clerk."

Nuju simply stared at the floor. For one used to the unlimited view from atop a Knowledge Tower, being confined like this was . . . disturbing. "We will never escape," he said. "Our freedom is gone. Our future is hopeless."

"Toa, giving up hope?"

The words came from a darkened corner of the cell. All three Toa Metru started in surprise — they had never imagined someone else was in the cell with them. Now they could see a lone figure sitting in a meditative pose, head down. He wore a robe with an oversized hood that hid his mask. But the experience and wisdom evident in his voice told them this must be a Turaga. But who? And why was he here?

"Turaga? Forgive me, but I know you not," said Nuju.

"Your concern should be with your own identity, not mine," the Turaga said quietly. "Freedom and escape are different objectives, but both are easily realized."

"With all respect, wise one," replied Onewa, "you are stuck in here with us, so —"

"I have freedom even in here," said the Turaga. "But for escape . . . Toa mask powers are needed."

The Toa exchanged glances. Whatever hope they had felt on encountering the mysterious Turaga was fading fast. "I doubt we will ever be in touch with our mask powers," said Nuju.

"Never doubt what you are capable of," answered the Turaga. "The Great Spirit lives through all of us."

Trapped in a cell with two Toa wannabes and a crazy Turaga, thought Onewa. *Next time some-one gives me a Toa stone, I think I will just use it as a doorstop.*

The Vahki transport crawled through the Sculpture Fields of Po-Metru. Its final destination remained a mystery, but at this point the farther the Toa were from the Coliseum, the more comfortable they felt.

In the back of the transport, Vakama had

succeeded in merging three of the six Great Disks. Using his firestaff, he had begun to shape the combined disks into the rough shape of a mask. Nokama watched him at work for a long time before saying, "Vakama, your destiny no longer lies in sculpting masks. You are a Toa."

Vakama shrugged. "I don't feel like a Toa."

"You will. Have faith."

As the Vahki transport went around a sharp curve, the three Toa Metru leaped out. They were well inside Po-Metru now and there was no point risking discovery by the Vahki at the wheel. They tumbled to safety and stayed low until the transport was out of sight. Then Nokama rose and looked around.

"An assemblers' village," she said, although it was obvious to all where they were. The village consisted of a broad avenue and a series of buildings. Scattered about were machines, furniture and statues, all of them half-finished. That was normal for such a place, but something else set the Toa on edge.

The village was abandoned. Doors banged open and closed in the wind. Tools lay where they had been dropped. Vakama's eyes narrowed as he noticed a stack of silver spheres near one of the buildings.

This place feels wrong-bad, thought Matau. "Hello?" he shouted.

No one answered.

Puzzled, he turned to Nokama and said, "Guess they all quick-sped."

"Builders do not abandon their projects without good reason," said the Toa of Water.

"Then where is everyone?" asked Vakama.

Krekka burst out of one of the buildings, launching energy bolts at the Toa Metru. "Get ready to find out, Toa!" he bellowed.

Nokama whirled, spinning her hydro blades fast enough to deflect the bolts. Then all three Toa dove for cover behind one of the buildings. But they had hardly hit the ground before Matau was ready to charge back out again.

"A Toa-hero knows no fear!" he said as he raced into the street. Krekka's next blast missed him, and the Toa of Air crowed, "You'll have to do better than that!"

Nidhiki accepted the challenge. Stepping out from behind a building, he hurled an energy web at the Toa. Entangled, Matau hit the ground.

"Help! There's a Toa down!" he yelled, struggling to get free.

Hearing his cry, Vakama and Nokama began to circle around the buildings to come to his aid. Meanwhile, Nidhiki and Krekka had both closed in on the captured Toa.

"Calling all Toa!" Krekka shouted. "Your time is up!"

A rapidly growing rumble drowned out anything else he said. The ground beneath their feet began to shake violently. "Bioquake?" suggested Vakama.

Now a cloud of dust had appeared on the far edge of the village, closing in on the Toa and Dark Hunters. From out of that cloud emerged a herd of fearsome beasts. Large bipeds, their powerful hind legs propelled them forward in huge leaps and bounds. Twin tusks on their lower jaws made the herd look like a spiked wall on the march. Their eyes burned red and deep roars came from their mouths as they stormed through the village.

"Worse!" said Nokaka. "Kikanalo!"

The eyes of the Dark Hunters went wide as they saw the herd bearing down upon them. Kikanalo were known for their stampedes, but were tolerated because their tusks often dug up chunks of protodermis left over from carving projects. Right now, though, their efficiency as recyclers was the last thing on anyone's mind.

"I hate those things!" said Krekka. His massive form moved amazingly fast as he scrambled to the top of a nearby tower. "I'm outta here."

"No!" yelled Nidhiki. "Stay low!"

But Krekka wasn't listening, and Nidhiki had no more time to worry about him. He dove into a construction trench as the herd thundered closer.

Matau struggled to his feet just as the Kikanalo entered the village. The force of their footfalls sent him flying through the air, to land with a crash near Vakama and Nokama. They darted out and dragged their dazed comrade into a small building.

Now the Kikanalo had made it as far as Krekka's tower. Almost casually, a few of the beasts rammed the tower with their tusks, sending it toppling over. Nidhiki looked up in time to see his partner and the structure falling right toward him.

"Next time, listen to me," he muttered.

Nokama saw Krekka land on top of Nidhiki in the ditch. Using her hydro blades, she cut loose a stack of the strange silver spheres and sent them rolling toward the ditch. Then she ducked back inside as the spheres crashed into the Dark Hunters.

Matau and Vakama watched the Kikanalo trampling and smashing assemblers' huts to bits. "We should quick-flee," said the Toa of Air.

"Nonsense," Nokama replied. "This is the sturdiest structure in the village."

"Nokama —" Vakama began.

The Toa of Water cut him off. "We're staying —"

Suddenly, three Kikanalo crashed through the ceiling of the building. Finding themselves closed in, the beasts panicked and began leaping wildly about, slamming into the Toa again and again. In desperation, Matau grabbed Nokama and Vakama and hurled them out the window before following himself.

He had acted just in time. Behind them, the building exploded as the angry Kikanalo kicked it to pieces. Once free, they leaped away to join the herd.

Nokama looked at Matau. "I was wrong. You were right, my brother."

"It's amazing what you can learn when you're not always speak-teaching," Matau replied.

The approach of more Kikanalo ended the argument as the Toa fled. They were barely staying ahead of the beasts, whose tusks swiped dangerously close to the three heroes. The lead beast was an aged Kikanalo, his hide covered with strange markings and old scars. He gave an impatient snort as he tried to catch up to the Toa Metru.

"What did you say?" Nokama asked Matau.

"I didn't —"

Matau stopped in midsentence. Nokama's mask had become illuminated, but the Toa of Water did not seem to notice. "Why is the mask glowing?" he asked.

Then Nokama did the most amazing, shocking thing Matau could ever imagine, under the circumstances: she stopped running. She simply stopped, with a Kikanalo stampede practically on top of her.

"Nokama?" Vakama shouted.

But she was paying no attention to him. She turned to face the onrushing beasts as if they were nothing to fear. Vakama and Matau both winced, sure the herd was about to trample their fellow Toa. The lead Kikanalo gave out an angry snort as it closed in on Nokama.

The Toa of Water responded with a similar sound. The lead Kikanalo, looking stunned, stopped with his tusks mere inches from her mask. The other beasts stopped as well, not in a pileup but like a well-drilled Vahki squad.

The elder Kikanalo's scars began to glow. He snorted aggressively at the Toa who stood before him. Nokama stared into his eyes as a new world opened up for her.

Turning back to the Toa, she said excitedly, "Brothers — my mask power! The chief wants to know why we are allied with Dark Hunters."

Vakama could not believe what he was hearing. Could Nokama really understand what these creatures were saying? Or had his visions finally driven sanity from him? No, this seemed real. Certainly his body ached enough from being thrown out a window onto the street.

"Tell him we're not," he said to Nokama. "We seek a friend the Hunters have taken."

Nokama turned her attention back to the Kikanalo chief and gave a series of animalistic grunts and snorts. The elder beast responded in kind, his body language relaxing.

"You are free to pass," Nokama translated, "since we are both against the Hunters who trespass the beauty of the Herdlands . . ."

"Beauty? Where?" Matau asked Vakama. "And who knew Kikanalo could think-talk? I just thought they were dumb beasts."

The elder Kikanalo grunted. Nokama chuckled as she reported, "Kikanalo still think the same of tall green Matoran."

"Tall Matoran?" said Matau, shocked. "I am Toa!"

"Wait," broke in Vakama, with barely contained excitement. "Tall Matoran? Ask him if the Dark Hunters trespassed with a 'tall Matoran.'"

Nokama nodded and translated Vakama's question into the language of the Kikanalo. The Rahi beast responded with a snort.

"Yes," Nokama said. "They take many things to the 'place of unending whispers.'"

"That must be where they have taken Toa Lhikan!" said Vakama.

The elder Kikanalo grunted, as if in agreement. "They will show us the way," Nokama translated.

The three Toa rode across the plains of Po-Metru on Kikanalo. Behind them, the rest of the herd followed close behind. For the first time, Vakama felt some hope. If they could find Lhikan, rescue him, surely Dume could be stopped. The Toa of Fire had no idea what the Turaga's plans were, or why he had turned against the city, but he had no doubt Lhikan could make things right.

Matau smiled. This was the sort of adventure he had always dreamed of during the long days riding Ussal crabs through Le-Metru. New places, new excitement, a quest to save a captured hero — this was what being a Toa-hero was all about! Laughing, he stood up on the back of the Kikanalo and started spinning around.

"Only a great Toa-rider could tame a wild Kikanalo-beast!" he proclaimed.

The Rahi's response was to stop and buck,

tossing the Toa of Air onto the ground. Matau landed with a hard thud.

"It seems a 'great Toa-rider' has been tamed," said Nokama. She and Vakama both smiled at the sight of Matau sprawled on the plain.

It would be the last time either one would smile for a long while.

Whenua had lived in dim light, sometimes almost complete darkness, for much of his life. Like any Onu-Matoran, over time his eyes had adjusted to the point where he could see in the semidark. Although much of Onu-Metru was on the surface, Onu-Matoran actually preferred to be in the underground levels of the Archives, because the brightness of the twin suns hurt their sensitive eyes.

Still, nothing had prepared him for the task at hand — trying to make his way around a small cell with a blindfold on. He kept bumping into walls and other Toa, and his temper was coming to a boil faster than protodermis in a Ta-Metru furnace.

The mysterious Turaga was not helping matters any. "Do not rely on your memory," he said. "Look beyond your history and see what is."

Look beyond history? Whenua had been an archivist — he lived for history! Telling an Onu-Matoran to forget about the past was like telling a Ko-Matoran to put away the telescope and lighten up.

"I'm not a Rahi bat!" snapped Whenua. "I can't see in the dark."

The Turaga quietly slid a stool into the path of the Toa of Earth. Whenua promptly tripped over it and hit the ground.

Onewa had been watching the whole exercise from his seat on the stone floor. Now he burst out laughing. "Soon you'll be ready for a game of pin the tail on the ash bear, record-keeper."

On the other side of the room, Nuju had spent the last hours transferring stones from one large pile to another. It was exhausting work, made all the more so by the fact that he could not see the point of it. How was hauling rocks going to make him a better Toa?

"I could toil at this task forever and still

learn nothing for the future," the Toa of Ice com-
plained.

The Turaga shook his head. "You could
learn that building the most noble tower begins
with the placement of a single stone."

Onewa chuckled. "Build a tower? A thinker
would never lay hands on stone. They're too busy
with their heads in the stars."

The Turaga turned to Onewa, smiling. "A
Toa's duty is to all Matoran, regardless of metru.
So you shall help both your brothers."

Onewa's smile faded, replaced with a dark
scowl. The Turaga extended his hands to the Toa
of Stone. In one, he held a rock; in the other a
blindfold.

Dawn was breaking over Po-Metru. As the twin
suns shed their light on the canyons, Matau,
Nokama, and Vakama lay flat on a ridge, survey-
ing the territory. For Toa used to the crowds
and tall buildings of their metrus, this place was
unsettling. Barren, largely uninhabited, its most

striking feature was the way echoes emanated from the canyon. It made it seem as if a thousand voices were speaking at once, in tones too low to hear.

The Kikanalo elder grunted. Nokama translated, "The place of unending whispers."

Down below, twenty Vahki Zadakh from Po-Metru guarded an entrance to Onu-Metru. Powerful and aggressive, they would not shrink from a fight with a thousand Toa, let alone three. Worse, one bolt from their tools and a victim became so suggestible that he or she would accept orders from anyone. Anyone who got stunned by a Zadakh could be made to turn on friends in an instant.

"Too many to rush," said Nokama.

"I have a plan. Perhaps we could . . ." Vakama began.

Onewa was having an even harder time moving blindfolded than Whenua. Po-Metru carvers relied on their vision and were used to laboring in the bright light of the suns. Darkness was a new world for him, and not one he particularly liked.

He turned in the wrong direction and slammed right into Whenua. The Toa of Earth ripped off his blindfold and turned on this Turaga.

"That was a complete waste of time!" Whenua shouted.

"Without self discovery, you will never find your destiny," the Turaga replied calmly. "It is every Toa's duty to the Great Spirit."

"This whole thing was a load of 'duty,' if you ask me," muttered Whenua.

Onewa stripped off his blindfold. Strangely, he did not seem angry or upset about having to participate in the exercise. "Sit down, Whenua," he said.

The Toa of Earth whirled to face him. "Taking orders from a Turaga was one thing, but from an overgrown hammer-swinger?"

For a moment, the two Toa's eyes were locked on each other. Then Onewa's mask began to glow. Whenua's eyes were glowing now as well, mirroring the look of the Mask of Power. Whenua tried to take a step forward and found that his feet would not move. A second later, he sat down, hard, on the floor, like a puppet whose strings had been cut.

"That's it," he seethed. "You're history, builder, even if I don't know how you did that!"

Whenua struggled to rise, arms reaching out to grab hold of Onewa. Nuju frowned at the spectacle of Toa fighting among themselves and snapped, "Stop! Now!"

Now the Toa of Ice's mask was glowing as well. Suddenly, great stones tore loose from one wall of the prison cell. The rocks flew rapidly across the room to form a wall between Onewa and Whenua. Moreover, they had left a sizable gap in the wall, perfect as an escape route.

All three Toa stood there, stunned by the turn of events. Then Nuju and Onewa both spoke at once, saying, "Your mask is glowing — your mask power!"

The Turaga simply gestured to the newly

made hole in the wall. "I believe the time has come to leave," he said.

Vahki were rarely, if ever, surprised by anything. After years of tracking down and subduing Rahi of all sorts, the order enforcement squads were experienced at handling almost any situation. Add to that foiling the ingenious attempts by some Matoran to try and take unscheduled vacations from work — one Ta-Matoran, Takua, practically rated an entire Nuurakh squad to himself — and Vahki could safely be said to have seen it all.

But even their visual receptors widened at the sight of Nokama emerging from the hills riding a Kikanalo. Vahki were trained to track, apprehend, and pacify. They were not accustomed to their targets coming to them.

Still, they wasted no time in responding to the Toa Metru's apparent insanity. One squad of Zadakh, stun staffs at the ready, broke off and pursued her. Even as they departed, a second squad spotted Matau on his beast and immediately gave chase. Despite the Zadakh's speed, the Kikanalo's knowledge of the terrain and greater agility allowed him to outdistance the pursuers.

Then came yet another shock for the Vahki. Instead of continuing to run, Matau and his mount suddenly pivoted, reversed course, and charged. "Aha! Toa never quick-flee!" shouted the Toa of Air.

The Vahki responded with blasts from their stun staffs, but the fast-moving Kikanalo leaped over and around the energy bolts. Nor did he show any signs of stopping as he plowed into the Vahki squad, his powerful legs slamming into the enforcers and sending them flying.

Matau smiled broadly as he saw the Vahki falling before his charge. He stood up on the back of the Kikanalo, saying, "Hey, Kikanalo, who's your mas —"

The Rahi looked up at him and gave a warning snort. Matau decided "master" probably wasn't the best term to use with a beast that could scatter Vahki like proto dust in a windstorm. "I meant who's your partner?" he said, quickly sitting back down.

Vakama had left his Kikanalo behind and approached the area on foot. He had hoped Nokama and Matau would have distracted all the Vahki from the entrance, but instead he rounded a corner to find three enforcers waiting for him. Their stun staffs blazed away. Vakama loaded and launched disk after disk, blocking each bolt at it came near. Still, he knew he would run out of Kanoka disks long before the Vahki ran out of power.

Rescue came from above. The elder Kikanalo leaped and landed in between the Toa of Fire and the Vahki. Glaring at the enforcers, he let out a long, low cry. Other Kikanalo emerged from the rocks and joined in the strange sound. It grew louder and louder as more of the Rahi added their voices to the chorus. For a moment, Vakama was convinced he must be going mad — the cry actually seemed to be reaching down into the ground and disturbing the rock.

No, it wasn't madness, he realized. It was

really happening. The cry had created a wave in the rocky surface of Po-Metru, which swept quickly toward the Vahki. It struck like a thunder-clap, hurtling the enforcers out of sight.

High on a ridge, Nokama was facing her own problems. She and her Kikanalo had backed up all the way to the edge of a cliff. The Vahki squad was pressing hard. The Toa of Water's hy-dro blades flashed in the sunlight as she deflected their stun blasts. If the enforcers were frustated by this, they gave no sign, instead continuing to march forward.

Nokama didn't need to look back. She knew that one more step by the Kikanalo would send them both plunging to their doom. She hoped the Great Spirit had seen to it that Vakama and Matau had been more successful.

The Toa of Water braced herself. The Vahki charged.

A split second later, a squad of Vahki were hanging on for their lives from the edge of the cliff. They had moved forward at full speed to capture a Toa, but when they got there, the

Legends of Metru Nui

Kikanalo jumped high into the air and out of their reach. Unable to stop themselves, the Vahki ran right off the cliff. The Kikanalo returned to earth with a thud.

The Vahki won't fall for that trick twice. They never do. And they won't give up, either, Nokama thought as she rode down from the ridge. *I hope the Kikanalo realize the kind of enemies they have made this day.*

Krekka and Nidhiki had arrived in time to see Matau's strategy bring down a Vahki squad. Krekka was still furious at the Kikanalo over the incident in the assemblers' village and wanted to bring the Rahi down. Nidhiki had to explain to him, more than once, that their job was to capture Toa, not dumb beasts.

The insectlike Dark Hunter pointed down to where Matau stood alone on the rocky plain. "Circle right," he ordered. Krekka nodded and moved off as Nidhiki headed to the left.

With some difficulty, Krekka made his way down into the box canyon. He didn't understand

79

why it was necessary to sneak up on the little green Toa — better to just charge in and tackle him. *Yeah,* he said to himself. *That's the thing to do. I'll drag him back to Nidhiki by his mask.*

Matau had wandered behind some rocks. Krekka smiled and charged, already imagining how the Toa would beg for mercy. But when he reached the boulders, it wasn't Matau who was waiting there, but Krekka's partner.

"Nidhiki?" Krekka asked, mystified. "Where'd the Toa go?"

"You must've let him slip past," snapped the other Dark Hunter. "Circle the other way back."

Krekka turned and left. He couldn't for the life of him figure out how Matau could have gone behind those rocks and then disappeared. He would have been even more puzzled if he had looked over his shoulder and seen a second Nidhiki approaching in the distance.

When that Nidhiki reached the rocks, it was to see what appeared to be Krekka standing around doing nothing. "Where is the Toa?" Nidhiki demanded.

Krekka shrugged.

"You let him get by you?"

"Maybe he got by *you*," rumbled Krekka.

Nidhiki turned away, muttering something about Dark Hunters who weren't bright enough to come in out of a rockslide. Once he was gone, the "Krekka" he had been speaking to morphed into Matau, his mask glowing with Toa power.

"Shapeshifting!" said the Toa of Air. "Some mask powers are worth waiting for!"

Matau mounted his Kikanalo and rode out of the canyon.

Krekka and Nidhiki spotted each other across the canyon. Both began shouting at once.

"Where's the Toa?"

"How should I know?"

"You told me to go the other way!"

"I told you to go that way!"

The canyon turned their voices into more of the "unending whispers" for which it was famous, the echoes of their argument carrying a long way.

*   *   *

The sounds reached the audio receptors of the last remaining Zadakh, but they were too busy to pay any attention. Snarling Kikanalo surrounded the squad, moving inexorably forward and kicking up a huge cloud of dust in the process. For a long moment, nothing was visible through the dust and the air was filled with Kikanalo snorts. When the cloud finally cleared away, the Vahki lay heaped in a pile.

Nokama and Vakama rode past them. Vakama was still tinkering with the Mask of Power he had created from the Great Disks. They were joined a moment later by Matau.

The elder Kikanalo grunted at Nokama. The Toa of Water dismounted and turned to her fellow Toa. "The chief said not bad . . . for flat-walkers. They will cover our herd tracks." Then she expressed her thanks to the elder in the language of the Kikanalo.

"Toa Lhikan will be forever in your debt," Vakama said to the elder beast.

Matau had dismounted as well and moved

to say good-bye to his Kikanalo. The Rahi acted first, giving the Toa a big, sloppy lick on his mask. "Arrgh!" Matau yelled, backing away.

With the Vahki defeated or driven off, it was now safe to enter the cave. Vakama put his project away and joined the other two as they entered the darkness of the cave. Behind them, the Kikanalo herd used their powerful legs to start a rockslide that sealed the cavern shut. Satisfied that they had blocked any pursuit of the Toa, the herd moved off.

None of the beasts chanced to look up in the sky. If they had, they would have seen the form of a lone Rahi hawk circling above the canyon. After a few more moments, Nivawk wheeled and soared toward the center of the city, carrying precious information for Turaga Dume.

7

Onewa, Whenua, Nuju, and their Turaga friend peered cautiously out of the opening in their cell wall. They had expected to see the barren plains of Po-Metru, but instead it seemed they were a long way from the outdoors. Their cell was inside a huge underground cavern, resting on an island of its own in the middle of a sea of sand. Stranger still, the cavern was empty — no patrols, no slobbering Rahi ready to hunt down escapees, no one.

"Why aren't there Vahki guards?" asked Onewa. The silence unnerved him. Somehow, the Toa of Stone felt they were in worse danger now than when they had been locked up.

The Turaga did not make him feel any better. "Perhaps none are needed," the wise one said, a hint of warning in his voice.

Still, an escape is not an escape if one never

leaves the cell. The four allies slipped through the gap and began trudging across the sand dunes. It was tough going for the Toa Metru, for their added weight caused their feet to sink deep in the sand.

They had been journeying only a short time when they saw the sand up ahead begin to move. What began as a subtle shifting of sand grains rapidly evolved into a huge dune coming right for them, accompanied by a monstrous groan.

"Now I know why!" said Nuju, as he and the others fled. But there was no way to run far enough or fast enough to outrace what was chasing them.

Behind the Toa, a massive form broke through the sand. The huge, horned, wormlike beast was known as a troller, and it was one of the most feared creatures in Po-Metru. It lived far beneath the sands, emerging only now and then to feed. No Po-Matoran had ever stayed in the vicinity of a troller long enough to find out just what it ate. But its gaping mouth was large enough to swallow an entire block in a metru.

Onewa felt the hot, fetid breath of the troller on his back. He turned to see its jaws about to close on him. Unbidden, his Mask of Power glowed once more.

High above the Coliseum, Nivawk circled once, twice, three times before swooping down. The Rahi hawk alighted on his perch in the sundial chamber.

"What news, Nivawk?" asked Turaga Dume.

The great bird screeched and squawked, speaking in a language Dume had mastered ages ago. He reported that Vakama, Matau, and Nokama had defeated the Vahki guards and were even now making their way into the prison cave.

Turaga Dume moved to the darkest corner of the room. A pair of red eyes stared at him from the shadows. "This mask has been useful," said Dume. "Now for its final task."

Dume took a step forward into the darkness. Nothing blocked his way, for there was no one else in the chamber. Only a shadowed mirror from which Dume's true face reflected back at him. Dume reached up and peeled off his Kanohi Mask of Power, to reveal another underneath — a twisted, blackened Mask of Shadows.

The guise of Metru Nui's Turaga had been cast aside, simply another mask to be removed. In his place stood an entity of darkness and destruction, and now the ultimate power in the city of legends.

"No one must alter our destiny," rumbled the dark figure.

The face of Turaga Dume appeared on kinetic displays all over the city. Matoran paused in their work to pay attention to what their elder had to say.

"Matoran of Metru Nui," the Turaga began. "You are required to gather at the Coliseum."

The troller slowly made its way to the rocky "coast" of the sea of sand. It swerved neither left nor right, even when small Rahi ran across its path. With a mighty heave, the beast beached itself and then opened its mouth as if in a yawn.

Three Toa and a Turaga emerged from the maw of the monster, gasping for air. Whenua turned to Onewa, saying, "Good job, brother. But next time, mind control something with better breath."

A tunnel led from the sand pit to a destination none of them could guess. But if they wanted to escape before any Vahki patrols came to investigate, they had no other choice. They would have to take their chances in the darkness.

At least we don't have to go in there without our tools, thought Onewa. All of their equipment was stacked neatly by the tunnel entrance, including a compact item that the Turaga took for himself. Onewa found that it felt good to have his proto pitons in his hands once more. He vowed that no one would ever take these symbols of his Toa power away again.

Nuju turned from the tunnel entrance. "All that lies ahead is shadow."

"It has to be better than what's behind us," said Whenua.

The Toa of Earth took a step into the dark

tunnel. Then he stopped in surprise — the tunnel was suddenly bright as day! How was this possible? He didn't see any lightstones anywhere, and he was certain none of the other Toa had one.

He turned back to check. The other Toa winced as if from glare. That was when Whenua realized they were brightly lit too. It was his mask! His mask was glowing and lighting the way in front of him!

"Your mask power," said Onewa.

"Come on," replied Whenua, smiling. "Our future just got a whole lot brighter."

Together, the three Toa and the Turaga entered the tunnel. The darkness vanished before them, something they hoped was an omen for the days to come.

They had been walking for some time through a strange tunnel lined with doors on either side. A faint sound came from around a sharp corner, something like metal scraping against stone. Whenua turned to his companions and signaled for them to stay put while he investigated.

The Toa of Earth rounded the corner and ran right into a Vahki coming the other way. The glow from Whenua's mask blinded the guard, giving the Toa an opening, and the two grappled. Whenua expected to be able to overcome a Vahki with his Toa power, but this one seemed unusually strong.

Then the Vahki did something totally unprecedented and unexpected — it talked. "Hey! Turn out the bright-light!"

Stunned, Whenua released his hold. Vahki couldn't talk . . . and that voice was familiar. "Matau?!"

The Vahki enforcer smiled — another thing no Vahki had ever done — and morphed into the form of the Toa of Air. "*Toa* Matau to you, my brother," he said.

Reunited, the Toa exchanged greetings and brief accounts of their adventures that brought them to the tunnels. Only Vakama stood off to the side, reluctant to join in the celebration.

"Shapeshifting?" Whenua asked Matau.

"Yeah," said the Toa of Air. "And you should hear Nokama translating Kikanalo."

"So we've all discovered our mask powers." No one noticed Vakama hang his head at Whenua's statement.

Nuju turned to Nokama. "How did you know we would be here?"

"We didn't. We came for Toa Lhikan."

Onewa shook his head. "Toa Lhikan is not here."

The Turaga took a step forward, saying, "Not exactly."

All eyes turned to his small form as he removed his cloak. For the first time, the others saw that he wore the same mask as Lhikan. In that moment, they knew — despite his reduced stature and power, this *was* —

"Toa Lhikan?!" Vakama said, shocked.

The Turaga smiled. "No, you are Toa. I am Turaga Lhikan."

"Why didn't you tell us who you were?" asked Whenua.

"Your task was to discover who *you* are," replied Turaga Lhikan. "Only with such knowledge would your powers reveal themselves."

"Fast-stop!" said Matau. "Where did — ?"

"My power go?" Lhikan finished for him. "It lives on, in all of you."

Vakama turned away, but Lhikan spoke directly to the Toa of Fire. "Tell me, the heart of Metru Nui, you have it safe?"

"Well . . . we're rescuing you now," Vakama answered, sounding a little confused by the question.

Lhikan sighed. "You are misguided, Toa Vakama. I am not Metru Nui's heart. The Matoran are. We must save them before it's too late."

Nokama turned to the Toa of Fire. "Vakama?"

"I have failed you again," Vakama said to Lhikan. Seeing the concern in Nokama's face, he snapped, "I told you I am a cross-wired freak, chasing his dreams, wasting everyone's time! I'm not a Toa! I'm not even a good mask-maker."

Further discussion was cut off by the sound of marching feet in the tunnels. It didn't take the wisdom of a Turaga to figure out what they belonged to.

"Vahki!" said Matau. "Run now, talk later!"

The group took off down a side corridor, Vakama bringing up the rear. They passed a number of huge doors, of the sort normally seen in the Archives. No one could imagine what purpose they would serve in Po-Metru.

Nokama paused to wait for Vakama to catch up. Lhikan shook his head and gestured for her to continue with the others.

"We cannot help Vakama," he said. "He needs to see the dignity in his own reflection. Only then will his destiny reveal itself."

Behind them, Vakama stopped short. His eyes had spotted something the other Toa had missed, something disturbingly familiar. It was a silver sphere, just like the ones he had seen in the Vahki transport.

Vakama wiped away the dust and opened the sphere. The hatch rose with a hydraulic hiss, to reveal . . .

"Turaga Dume?" Vakama said, shaken to the core of his being. But there was no escaping it — there was the Turaga, minus his mask, sleeping inside the vessel. In his heart, Vakama knew this was no ordinary sleep and Dume would not be roused with a shake.

Lhikan looked over his shoulder at Vakama. "The true Turaga Dume. As I feared, an impostor is posing as a mask we all trust."

The world spun around Vakama. He knew the Turaga had been behaving oddly, but he never suspected . . . Another vision assailed his senses. Hundreds of silver spheres . . . sinister red eyes . . . whispered words that spoke of evils yet to come.

The other Toa had turned back at the news. "If this is Turaga Dume . . ." said Onewa.

"You don't want to know who is in control of Metru Nui," Vakama replied.

The sounds of Vahki on the march came from another corridor. The Toa Metru were about to be trapped between two order enforcement squads. Whenua looked around desperately, finally spotting their only avenue of escape.

"In here!" he yelled, pulling open one of the massive doors. The Toa and Turaga Lhikan rushed inside a split second before the Vahki reached the spot. Whenua slammed the door behind them. Frustrated, the Vahki pounded on it. The door rapidly began to give way before their might.

The Toa examined their surroundings. They were in a Po-Metru storage facility littered with tools, half-finished carvings, and one potential ticket to freedom. Matau was the first to spot it.

"A Vahki transport!" he shouted.

Although based on the same design as the one in which he, Nokama, and Vakama had hitched a ride before, this transport was even larger. Its insectoid legs looked as if they had not moved in an age, and certainly the thick coating of dust made it seem long unused. But Matau knew these vehicles well. Like the Vahki they carried, they never wore out.

He took a step toward the transport, but stopped dead at a hissing sound. It came from the darkest corner of the room. The Toa Metru were not alone, and they had the worst possible company.

"Lohrak!" shouted Turaga Lhikan, as the

hideous, winged serpents flew from the shadows. Their huge, powerful mouths were filled with row upon row of needlelike teeth, which gleamed in the light.

Lohrak were known, and feared, throughout Metru Nui. First discovered by Onu-Metru miners years ago, the creatures had spread all over the city. They were as territorial and aggressive as they were slimy and disgusting. Dwellers in darkness, they had proved to be a particular problem for archivists and maintenance workers. But every metru had Matoran who could share a frightening story of a Lohrak encounter.

Workers who wandered off the job to go exploring were warned that Lohrak might lurk anywhere. For a time, the creatures were even pronounced a protected species by Turaga Dume, in hopes of stopping digging projects that might unearth more of the monsters.

At the moment, though, it was the Toa who needed protection. The first Lohrak lunged at Whenua, who dove out of the way. Others had wrapped themselves around Turaga Lhikan and

Toa Nokama's hydro blades. Nuju struggled with his crystal spikes to pry two more of the beasts off his legs.

It was chaos. The Lohrak swooped and dove as the Toa desperately tried to dodge and regroup. Meanwhile, the Vahki continued trying to break down the door. Vakama, Matau, and Nuju finally managed to join together to form a united defense, but then all three were blinded by the radiance of Whenua's mask.

"Onewa, mind-control these things!" shouted the Toa of Earth.

Onewa concentrated, his mask beginning to glow. But the power of the Kanohi did not slow down the Lohrak's attack. "There are too many!" he said.

"Then do something else," said Whenua. "Some Toa we turned out to be."

"Someone must take charge," said Lhikan.

The words cut through the doubts that Vakama carried with him. Lhikan was right. If one of them did not take command, their struggle was going to end here in this dusty storage room.

There would be no one to warn the Matoran, to stop Dume, or to bring Nidhiki and Krekka to justice.

I have been all wrong, he said to himself. *A Toa is not someone who has no fear — but someone who masters their fear. Toa can doubt, and worry, and question, just like a Matoran. But in the end, a Toa must act.*

"You found your mask powers!" he shouted to the other Toa. "Now remember your elemental powers!"

It was a desperate gamble and he knew it. The Toa had used up most of their elemental powers in the quest to find the Great Disks. None of them knew for sure how long it would take the powers to recharge. What if they had not come back yet?

Only one way to know-learn, thought Matau. Shouting "Wind," he raised his aero slicers, unleashing a blast of wind just strong enough to blow the Lohrak off himself, Nokama, Lhikan, Vakama, and Whenua.

Nokama followed his lead. Using her hydro

blades, she hurled a blast of water at Nuju and Onewa, scattering the Lohrak that besieged them. "Water!" she cried triumphantly.

"We need to trap them," said Vakama.

Whenua and Onewa went to work. Using his earthshock drills, Whenua channeled his elemental power into the wall. His seismic forces cracked the stone, creating a gap almost big enough to hold the Lohrak. Onewa used his proto pitons to enlarge the opening and smooth the stone.

Vakama's elemental powers had not yet returned in force, but his mask-making tool was able to create enough heat and flame to drive the creatures into the gap. Once they were inside, Nuju sealed it shut with a layer of transparent ice. Behind the ice, the trapped Lohrak snapped their jaws angrily.

"We have our unity," said Vakama. "Now let's do our duty."

Behind him, the door began to crack under the relentless pounding of the Vahki. They would be through in a matter of seconds, and all hope of escape would be lost. More likely, the Toa Metru would wind up docile servants of order, happily laboring under the watchful eye of the Turaga Dume impostor.

The Toa climbed into the Vahki transport. As Matau had expected, getting it started was not difficult. But there was one other problem . . .

"Our only exit is blocked," said Whenua. He was right — the Toa had angry Vahki behind them, and a solid wall in front.

"Then we'll make our own," Vakama replied, new confidence in his voice. "Come on, destiny awaits."

"What about Turaga Dume?" asked Onewa.

"He'll be safe until we return," said Vakama. "Now go!"

The Vahki transport shot forward. Whenua stood on the hood, his earthshock drills revved up. The vehicle accelerated rapidly and the Toa watched as the solid stone wall came closer and closer. Whenua leaned forward a little, bracing for the moment his drills would strike stone.

Impact! The Toa of Earth's tools bore

through the rock with ease, digging an exit tunnel for the transport. Just as they exited the chamber, the door gave way and the Vahki poured in. They looked around, annoyed. Where had their quarry gone? Their orders were very specific: apprehend and pacify. But these Toa were proving hard to catch.

At the controls, Matau eased the vehicle upward as Whenua continued to dig. Soon they were riding up a gentle ramp, headed for the surface and freedom.

Matau turned to Nokama, smiling. "I see us taking a romantic ride-drive."

"And you believe Vakama has odd visions?" Nokama shot back.

8

The Vahki transport exploded out of the ground. Matau had been worried about the possibility of injuring Matoran when the vehicle hit the surface. Now he saw he need not have worried, because there were no Matoran in sight.

Anywhere.

For the first time, the Toa of Air wondered if they were going to be too late. They would go down in legend as the heroes who took too long to come to the rescue. Then again, if they weren't on time, there might not be anyone left to write the legends. He leaned on the throttle and rocketed the transport to the heart of the city.

Up front, Whenua collapsed, exhausted. He had never felt such complete and utter fatigue in his whole life, but it was a good feeling. It meant he had done his job and come through when the

Toa needed him most. Maybe he *could* do this job, after all.

Onewa leaned forward. "Hey, glow-head."

Whenua turned to look at him, bracing for another one of Onewa's insults. But instead the Toa of Stone held out a hand and said, "Well done, my brother."

Both Toa smiled and clanked their fists together.

Further back, Vakama was absorbed in mask-making once again. He couldn't explain why, but he had a strong feeling this mask he was making was going to be vital to saving the city.

If it can be saved, he thought. *Whoever is posing as Dume has Nidhiki, Krekka, and the Vahki on his side. Plus the Matoran believe him to be the city's elder and will follow his orders. I only hope they are not the last orders they ever follow.*

Matoran streamed into the Coliseum from all over the city, under the watchful optical sensors of the Vahki. Most looked confused, some looked worried, but a few were simply happy for a break from work. All of them had come in response to Turaga Dume's call. They had no idea what had prompted the city-wide alert, but they were sure it was nothing that Dume could not handle. After all, he was the Turaga, wasn't he?

The false Turaga Dume watched the unsuspecting Matoran file in. They were so innocent. They would never be able to handle the changes that were coming. Better that they should be sheltered from it all, until such time as he decided they could resume their lives again.

He turned to look at the massive sundial. The shadows of the twin suns had begun to partially overlap. Smiling, he glanced at a Kanohi Mask of Power that hung on the wall, the symbol of the Great Spirit Mata Nui.

"Ah, twilight," he whispered. "The dawn of shadows."

The Vahki transport sped through the streets of Metru Nui. None of the Toa Metru said a word as they traveled. They were all taking in the spectacle of a completely empty city. The streets, workplaces, and chutes were all deserted, almost as if no one had ever lived there. It was awe-inspiring and more than a little frightening.

On screens all over the city, the image of Turaga Dume hung like a shadow. He repeated the same words, over and over: "Matoran of Metru Nui are required to gather at the Great Coliseum for an important announcement."

Vakama turned to Turaga Lhikan. "Turaga, you said I must 'stop the darkness.' But sunsfall isn't for —"

"Just because the suns hang above us now does not mean that they will always burn bright," Lhikan replied.

Nuju and Whenua looked skywards to see the two suns arc toward each other. "Of course," said the Toa of Earth. "The legend of eternal shadow."

"When the light of the Great Spirit will be lost," said Nuju.

Nokama understood now, and it was worse

than she could ever have imagined. "We don't have much time!" she cried, not realizing that time had already run out.

Matoran sat expectantly in their seats, engaging in nervous conversation with each other. Then the huge Coliseum screen flared to life and the mask of Turaga Dume looked down upon them.

"Matoran, rejoice, for today will be a momentous climax to your history," he said, in a benevolent tone.

The Matoran looked at each other, puzzled. Their confusion grew as Vahki transports pulled into the arena, carrying scores of shiny silver capsules.

Matau steered the transport sharply around a corner and poured on the speed. The Coliseum was just up ahead, its entrance guarded by Vahki enforcers. "Grip-tight!" shouted the Toa of Air.

The Vahki realized too late that the vehicle was not going to stop. Startled, they dove aside as the transport smashed through the Coliseum

gates. Debris flew everywhere. Matau fought to
maintain control as the vehicle skidded across
the arena floor.

Come on, he said to himself. *You are a Toa-
hero! You are a Le-Metru star! You can stop one
quick-fast Vahki cart!*

He yanked back on the controls and the
rear of the vehicle whipped to the right before
finally sliding to a stop. But if Matau expected
applause from the audience of Matoran, he was
sadly mistaken. There were no Matoran in the
Coliseum . . . none that were conscious, anyway.
Shocked, the Toa Metru saw the Vahki closing the
last of the capsules, which now contained the
population of Metru Nui.

The Toa of Air shook his head. This could
not be right. There were nowhere near enough
capsules here to hold all of the Matoran. Where
were the rest of them?

A voice came from the giant screen, but it
was not the voice of Turaga Dume. It was a dark
sound that sent chills through the Toa. It was the
sound of shadow and fear, decay and rot, a cor-

ruption beyond anything the Toa could imagine. It was the growls of wild Rahi in the night, the hiss of angry Rahkshi, and the thunder that shook the ground, all entwined together in one terrible noise.

"Too late, Toa," the false Turaga said. "The shadow has arrived."

The Toa Metru looked up at the screen. "Turaga Dume" slowly reached up and removed his mask, revealing a pair of blazing red eyes and a face all too well-known to the heroes. Even in the shape of a Turaga, there was no denying the raw power that radiated from the figure. Once he had been a being trusted and respected by all, but now . . . now he was a stranger from the shadows.

Turaga Lhikan was the first to find his voice. "Makuta," he said, stunned. "You were sworn to protect the Matoran!"

"I shall," said Makuta. "And when they awake, *I* will be their Great Spirit."

Vakama could not believe what he was hearing. He knew there was a plot against the

Matoran, he knew that "Dume" was an impostor, but he had never dreamed of something so monstrous. How could Makuta — how could anyone — be so twisted and evil that he would try to take the place of the Great Spirit, Mata Nui?

"Deceit and self-interest will never be virtues the Matoran honor," the Toa of Fire spat.

A rumble began to grow, slowly at first, then faster, so loud it was deafening. Yet Makuta's voice could be clearly heard through the din, heavy with triumph. "How very bold. Now embrace the nightfall. Even the Great Spirit will soon sleep."

The Toa and Turaga lifted fearful eyes to the sky. A darkness passed over them, cutting off the light. Shadow reached down like a great hand to seize Metru Nui, engulfing the city in an all-consuming blackness. Midday had become midnight.

Forked lightning bolts stabbed down from the Coliseum's energy pylons. The ground shook violently as a spiderweb of cracks appeared in the walls. A great fissure appeared in the floor of the arena, racing toward the heroes.

The legend of eternal shadow had come true. The end of all was near.

Only the Vahki, heartless machines that they were, seemed unfazed by the disaster unfolding around them. Optical receptors aglow in the darkness, they marched toward the Toa's vehicle. Makuta obviously intended that there would be no loose ends left behind.

But worrying about their own safety was the last thing on the minds of the Toa. "We must find the Matoran!" yelled Vakama. "Whenua!"

Whenua nodded and concentrated as never before. His Mask of Power glowed as brightly as a sun, its light piercing the ground. Suddenly he was able to see through solid matter, his vision extending down into a storage hold far beneath the Coliseum. Vahki enforcers were busy stacking silver cylinders on huge metal racks that stretched from floor to ceiling.

"Below the Coliseum!" said Whenua.

The Toa of Air slammed on the controls,

throwing the transport into high gear. Vahki went flying as the Toa headed for an underground access tunnel. One Vahki managed to recover in time to leap and dig its tools into the rear of the transport, slowly starting to climb toward where the Toa sat.

Nokama turned and spotted the unwelcome guest. With a quick swipe of her hydro blades, she sliced off that section of the transport, sending the Vahki tumbling away.

Makuta triggered the controls that caused Dume's box to ascend. The energy pylons bent to his will, sending their lightning discharges into his body. He hungrily absorbed the raw energy into himself until it became too much for the frail form of a Turaga to bear.

The moment he had waited for — the moment of transformation — had arrived.

The transport roared through the tunnel. Three Vahki leaped from above as it passed, landing on the roof of the vehicle. They immediately began pounding with their tools to gain access.

Inside the cockpit, Matau flipped a lever. The transport's legs extended, lifting the vehicle up high. A second later, a "low bridge" stripped the Vahki off the top and sent them tumbling to the ground.

The transport slid to a stop in the middle of the storage facility. The Toa disembarked to view a horrifying sight. All around them were the silver spheres, stacked as high as the eye could see. Each one contained a Matoran who not so long ago had been laughing, working, playing.

Nokama peered inside one of the spheres. The Matoran within slept an unnatural sleep, eyes dark, heartlight faintly pulsating. He was still alive, at least, but trapped in a slumber which, for all the Toa knew, was endless.

"Can we save them all?" she asked.

"Time is too short," replied Vakama. "But if we save a few, we save hope for all."

The Toa hurriedly loaded six spheres into

the transport, all the while watching for Vahki. They could not know what was happening up above, but in their hearts they knew Makuta would not let them escape without a fight.

"Let's get them to safety," said Vakama.

High above the Coliseum, Makuta now reigned supreme. His frail Turaga form had been replaced by a swirling vortex of dark energy. The energy pylons continued to pour bolts of lightning into his new shape, feeding him the power he craved. Makuta's red eyes gleamed in the center of the shadow.

Nivawk circled the vortex, careful not to come too close. His caution was wasted, as a black tendril of pure energy reached out and dragged him into the swirling mass of darkness.

Hidden by the shadows, the Vahki transport accelerated away from the Coliseum. Matau struggled to keep the vehicle on the road as earth tremors rocked the city. Towers crumbled and chutes buckled and fell as they raced toward Ga-Metru.

Suddenly Krekka and Nidhiki were flanking the vehicle in their flight mode. Before any of the Toa could react, they had morphed back into their normal shapes and leaped into the vehicle. Krekka grabbed Matau, fighting him for control of the transport.

"Time for a new driver!" shouted the Dark Hunter.

Nidhiki ignored the Toa and made straight for Lhikan, his eyes filled with hate. "Toa or Turaga, Lhikan, your fate shall be the same."

Nidhiki launched an energy web at the Turaga, only to watch, astounded, as it slowed and then stopped in midair. Nearby, Nuju's mask glowed as he used his telekinetic power to halt the net.

Now it was Onewa's turn. He focused his power of mind control on Krekka, taking over the body of the Dark Hunter. Under Onewa's direction, Krekka whirled and grabbed hold of Nidhiki.

"Get off!" shouted Nidhiki.

"My thoughts exactly," Onewa muttered. With a mental shove, Krekka jumped off the speeding vehicle, taking his partner with him.

Lhikan smiled and clanked his fist with Onewa.

Nidhiki and Krekka shook their heads, trying to recover from the impact of hitting the road. Krekka had no idea how they had wound up there. The last thing he remembered, he was fighting the green Toa and winning.

Neither one noticed the coils of dark energy approaching. Then the shadow was around them both, dragging them back into the Coliseum to an unknown fate.

9

Matau steered the transport across the bridge leading to Ga-Metru. He tried his best to stay focused on the task at hand, and not pay attention to the damage being done to his beloved city.

"I always believed all this would stand forever," Nokama said sadly.

"Sometimes you shouldn't look back," answered Whenua. "Only ahead."

"Ahead does not appear so great either," said Nuju.

The Toa looked ahead to see hundreds of Vahki standing in the middle of the bridge. Twenty abreast, they blocked the way from rail to rail.

"Where to now?" said Matau.

Vakama had gone back to tinkering with the Mask of Power he was crafting. "Our future lies beyond Metru Nui," he said confidently.

Matau nodded. He wasn't sure what that meant, but he knew there was only one safe way to get off this bridge. "I sure hope you're guided by the Great Spirit," he growled, "because this is definitely cross-wired!"

The Toa of Air threw the transport into a hard ninety degree turn and sped toward the rail. The Toa hung on to whatever they could, hardly able to believe what was about to happen. With a final burst of speed, the transport smashed through the rail and plunged into the storm-tossed waters far below.

The Vahki gathered at the newly made gap in the rail and looked down. There were no signs of Toa or any wreckage of their vehicle. All that could be seen were the waves beating against the bridge supports as if they hoped to bring the structure crashing down.

Then a few bubbles popped to the surface, followed by the transport itself, still intact. The six spheres, strapped to the vehicle, had made it buoyant enough to rise. "We saved them," said

Nokama, pointing at the containers that held the sleeping Matoran. "Now they saved us."

Nidhiki and Krekka had no idea what was happening. They had served Turaga Dume faithfully, hadn't they? Even when it turned out it was not Dume at all, they had obeyed his orders without question. Why, then, were they now being drawn into the heart of a vortex of darkness?

"It is time you made good on your promises, my captains," Makuta said as the two vanished into the pulsating shadow. "For this is your eternal duty."

With its insectoid legs acting as oars, the Vahki transport moved through the silver sea. Up ahead lay the Great Barrier, a cliff so high it vanished into the sky and so wide it encompassed the entire horizon.

Vakama was paying no attention to the barrier though. His mind was lost in another vision. . . .

Bright light. Then darkness, the same kind of darkness that now shrouded all of Metru Nui. He looked around, uncertain, wondering how he would ever escape. Then a sliver of illumination appeared, like a crack in the shadows. It beckoned him to go forward, for on the other side was a place of safety. . . .

Vakama's eyes snapped open. He wasn't certain just what the vision meant, not yet, but he did know it was a sign of hope. That same instinct told him the Mask of Power he had been creating would play some part in all this, so he went back to work on it.

Matau looked on, disapprovingly. In the middle of this crisis, Vakama was still playing mask-maker? "It is time you realized you are a Toa," he said.

"Time? Of course!" said Vakama. "More time! That is what the false Turaga wanted!" Now he worked even more frantically on his mask. It was almost finished, and if he was right about what it could do —

Vakama's thoughts were interrupted by another violent tremor. But this one was not caused by thunder in the ground. No, this came from the impact of a winged figure landing hard on a rocky outcropping of the Great Barrier.

The Toa stared in wonder, in awe, in fear. This was unmistakably Makuta, but not Makuta as they had ever known him. This was a colossus in dark, infected armor, with the mighty wings of Nivawk, radiating the power of shadow. Worse, the Toa Metru could see that the tools of Nidhiki and Krekka were a part of his new form as well.

No wonder they stopped chasing us, thought Nuju grimly.

Makuta looked down upon the Toa. Over the crashing of the waves and the howling wind, he snarled, "Your journey must end."

"By the will of the Great Spirit, it has just begun!" roared Vakama.

"Then conquer the real sea of protodermis!" said Makuta.

With a wave of his arm, great pillars of crystalline protodermis rose from the sea, forming a dangerous obstacle course. Matau struggled with the controls as he steered the craft around them, but the Vahki transport was not designed for complicated maneuvers at sea.

Vakama pointed up ahead. There was a narrow gap in the Great Barrier through which light shone, just like the image he had seen in his vision. "Keep to the light, Matau. The future is in your care," he commanded. Then he turned to the Toa of Ice and said, "Get me as close to him as you can."

The Toa of Ice nodded as his mask began to glow. His telekinetic power reached out and lifted Vakama into the air, sending him hurtling up toward where Makuta waited.

Down below the Toa fought on. Onewa jumped from the craft to smash one pillar to fragments with his proto pitons. But two more rose up dead ahead, so close their spikes ground together. The transport was on course to smash into them.

"We need to quick-turn!" said Matau.

Nokama slung her hydro blade and dug it into the side of a pillar. Then she hung on with all her strength as Matau threw the transport into a sharp turn, narrowly avoiding the barrier up ahead. But victory had not been won — another pillar rose up abruptly, crashing into the transport and sending the silver spheres flying into the sea.

Nokama spotted them floating toward certain destruction. "The Matoran!"

Nuju saw them as well, and it broke his concentration just enough to send Vakama plunging into the sea. But the Toa of Fire was not ready to give up. He dragged himself from the water and scaled the cliffside to face Makuta.

The two circled each other warily. Vakama reached into his pack and produced the completed Mask of Power he had fashioned from the Great Kanoka disks.

"The Mask of Time," breathed Makuta. Then the master of shadows smiled. "You are a great mask-maker, Vakama. You could have many destinies."

Vakama hesitated. Makuta, sensing his doubt, moved in closer. "Fire and shadow are a mighty combination. Come join my brothers and I, Vakama."

The Toa of Fire smiled. "I desire but one noble destiny," he said, placing the Mask of Time over his own Kanohi mask. "More than any power you can offer me."

"Then accept your doom," thundered Makuta. He gathered his energies and sent a serpent-like stream of dark energy from his chest straight toward Vakama.

The Mask of Time glowed. A wave of temporal force flowed from it, striking Makuta. The movements of the master of shadows slowed, as did his energy stream, which now hung almost motionless in mid air.

Stripped of Makuta's control, the sea calmed. The five Toa down below quickly went to work retrieving the Matoran spheres. None of them noticed that Turaga Lhikan was missing.

Although he wore the Mask of Time, Vakama's control of it was imperfect. He was unable to stop the same temporal wave that slowed

Makuta from slowing himself as well. He could feel his mind and body slowing down — and now there was no way to dodge the tentacle of dark energy heading for him.

Then there was motion. Turaga Lhikan was running up to Makuta and Vakama, diving into the temporal wave right in front of Makuta's dark energy. The energy bolt struck Lhikan head on, shattering the shield created by his own mask. Lhikan was drained of all color as the darkness took hold. The disruption of the wave broke its power, and sent Vakama's Mask of Time flying into the sea.

Vakama knelt over the dying Turaga, saying, "That was meant for me."

"No," Lhikan responded weakly. He gestured toward the Great Barrier. "This is my lifetime's journey. Yours lies beyond."

Vakama struggled with the feeling of grief that threatened to overpower him. He leaned in close to hear Turaga Lhikan's whispered words.

"Trust your visions," the Turaga said. "I

125

am proud to . . . have called you brother . . . Toa Vakama."

With that, Lhikan's eyes went dark and his heartlight ceased to flash. Broken-hearted, Vakama removed the Turaga's mask, even as the shadow of Makuta fell upon him once more.

"Fool!" snapped Makuta. "Without the Mask of Time, it will take a lifetime to achieve what destiny demands. But your lifetime will be brief."

Makuta launched another tendril of dark energy at Vakama, forcing the Toa to scramble for safety. Then Vakama's mask suddenly began to glow, and his body faded from view. He had become invisible!

Makuta fired more blasts wildly, but missed the Toa by a wide margin. Vakama hurled a rock, sparking another blast from Makuta at the point where it landed. Then the master of shadows aimed at the point from which the rock came, his dark energy forcing Vakama into a hollow of the cliff.

The Toa of Fire removed his disk launcher

and wedged it hard into a crevice on the cliff face. As soon as the launcher was separated from him, it became visible. Makuta smiled and sent a tentacle of dark energy to grab it.

"You cannot hide from me, Toa!" said Makuta.

"I don't need to anymore," Vakama replied.

The shadow wrapped around the launcher and tried to pull it toward him — but Vakama had wedged it in too deeply. Makuta found himself struggling with the power of the Great Barrier itself. Instead of the launcher being drawn toward him, he was being drawn toward the Barrier.

Vakama returned to visibility as Makuta slammed into the cliff. Dazed, but still defiant, the dark one snarled, "If Toa Lhikan could not defeat me alone, how can you?"

"Because he is not alone!" The voice was Nokama's. The six Toa stood together once more.

The Toa raised their tools, with Vakama substituting his firestaff for his disk launcher. Their six elements flowed together to form a beam of pure white energy, which they hurled at Makuta, leeching his shadow power from him. A shell of protodermis formed around the master of shadows, sealing him in. With a final burst of power, the beam marked his prison with the sign of the Toa.

The Toa broke formation and the power beam ceased. Vakama looked at Lhikan's mask and saw the streak of a star reflected in it. "Look skyward!" he said.

The Toa turned their eyes to the heavens. Lhikan's spirit star was shooting across the darkened sky. As they watched, it exploded into six new stars.

"Six spirit stars . . ." said Vakama.

"The Great Spirit proclaims it!" said Nuju. "We are Toa!"

The six heroes raised their fists and clanked them together. Their trials were far from ended, they knew, but they would face them as heroes of Metru Nui.

Vakama looked down from the cliff to see that all six spheres had been retrieved and lashed once more to the transport. "We'll return for the rest of the Matoran soon," he said. "But first let us ensure the safety of those we have with us now."

Much time would pass before the Toa Metru would first set foot on the island that lay far beyond the Great Barrier. An even greater span of time would go by before they returned again with as many Matoran as they could rescue from Metru Nui. In that time, the Toa would fight many battles, make new allies and confront powerful new enemies. They would learn lessons about heroism and sacrifice that would never be forgotten.

Now, after so very long, they at last stood on the beach. Hundreds of silver spheres littered the sands. The Matoran within them still slept.

"Toa Lhikan sacrificed his power for us," said Vakama. "Now we shall do the same for them."

Vakama placed his hand on one of the capsules. His mask began to glow brightly.

"May the heart of Metru Nui live forever," he said solemnly.

Power flowed from him and the other Toa, spreading like a blanket of pure energy over the capsules. One by one, the eyes of the Matoran snapped open, their heartlights began to flash, as awareness returned to them. By the sacrifice of the Toa, they had been brought back to waking life.

The heroes looked at one another. They were Toa no longer — by giving up their power to save others, they had become six Turaga. They watched with happiness and pride as the spheres opened and the Matoran emerged.

"This is the island of Mata Nui, named in honor of the Great Spirit," proclaimed Vakama.

The Matoran looked around at the beach, the ocean, the trees — it was all so very new to them. One Matoran, Takua, ran up to Vakama and directed his attention to another. It was a Ta-Matoran named Jaller whose mask had been badly damaged in the transport.

Vakama looked at Turaga Lhikan's mask.

Then, smiling, he removed Jaller's damaged Kanohi mask and replaced it with Lhikan's. Rejuvenated, Jaller rose to join his friends. A Ga-Matoran named Hahli rushed to embrace him and welcome him to the Matoran's new home — the island of Mata Nui.

EPILOGUE

"And so it was as it is," said Turaga Vakama.
The assembled Turaga, Matoran, and Toa
Nuva looked on as he placed the stone that represented the Great Spirit in the center of the
sand circle once more.

"Matoran into Toa, Toa into Turaga, Turaga
into legend. Remembering deeds past and bringing hope to the future. United in duty. Bound in
destiny. This is the way of the Bionicle!"

And so it was, and so it ever shall be.